On a Dark, Dark Night

Written by Jean M. Cochran

Illustrated by Jennifer E. Morris

Text copyright Jean M. Cochran © 2009
Illustrations copyright Jennifer E. Morris © 2009

ISBN: 978-1-935025-00-9
Library of Congress Control Number: 2008924643

10 9 8 7 6 5 4 3 2 1

Published by Pleasant St. Press
PO Box 520
Raynham Center, MA 02768 USA
www.pleasantstpress.com
e-mail: info@pleasantstpress.com

Book Design by Jill Ronsley, suneditwrite.com

Printed and bound in the USA
Worzalla Publishing, 3535 Jefferson St., Stevens Point, WI 54481
Production Date: 082009
Run: 101436

To my father, Paul Jennette,
whose spooky stories kept my sisters and me
delightfully scared out of our wits.
–JMC

To Mike for putting up with me.
–JEM

On a dark, dark night
As black as pitch,
I thought I heard the
Cackle of a wicked witch.

He he he heeee

I sat up in my bed,

Put my feet on the floor,

When a dark, dark shadow
Passed by my door.

I stepped into the hallway,
Heard a *creak ... creak ... creak ...!*

Frightened in my flannels,
I took a little peek.

The witch had found my sister!
She'd slipped into her room.
My heart was a-poundin'
with a . . .

Boom!

Boom!

Boom!

I crept inside the closet. My bones shook with fright
From the witch on the prowl on that dark, dark night.

I heard the chimes a-ringin' on the hallway clock.
My knees were a-clankin' with a

Knock!

Knock!

Knock!

In the dark, dark closet,
My eyes could hardly see.
I heard the witch's footsteps comin'—
One! … Two! … Three!

Then *squeak* … *squeak* … *squeak* …
My little brother's door!
First she found my sister—
Now she wanted more.

Silent in my slippers, I snuck back to my room.

Leaning in the corner was the wicked witch's broom!

I shut the door behind me and dove into my bed,
Pulled the covers to my chin and up around my head.

Underneath my blankets,
I didn't make a peep.
I thought I'd trick the witch
'Cause she'd think I was asleep.

My door opened suddenly,
And standing in the hall
Was the wickedest of witches
With a shadow ten feet tall!

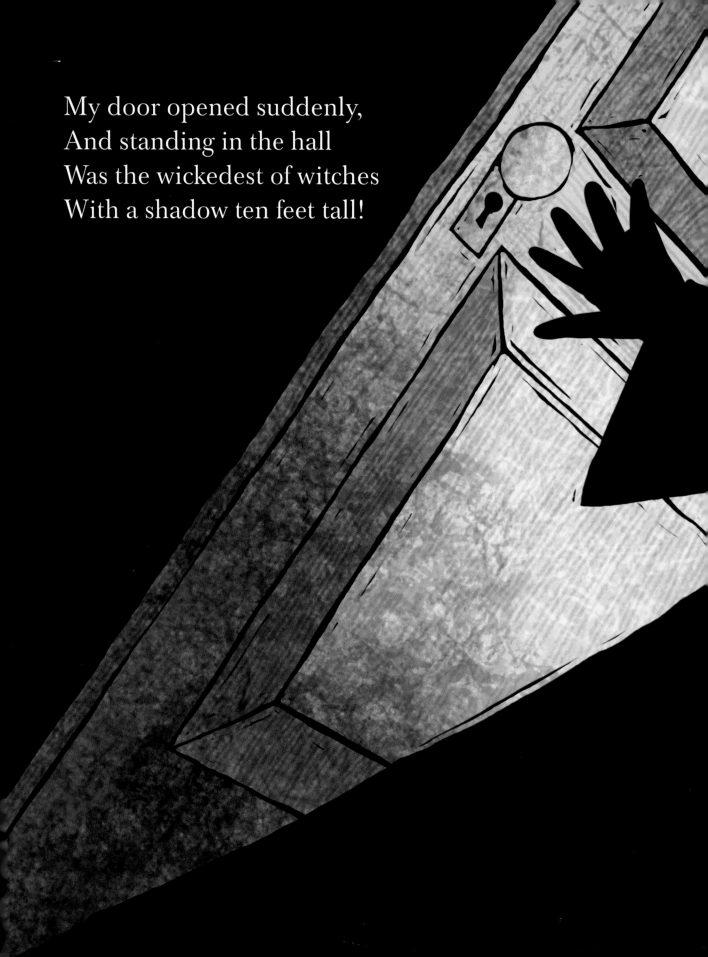

I opened one eye slightly as she slunk into my room,
Slithering like a snake and spreading doom and gloom.

She crouched beside my bed. My hands began to shake.
She flicked my bedroom light on . . .

and said . . .

Sitting in my bedroom was
MY MOTHER in her robe,
Wearing Daddy's cap
'Cause her head had gotten cold!

She kissed me on the cheek.
Then she tucked me in tight,

And I drifted off to sleep on that dark, dark night.